Gletta the Foal

written and photo-illustrated by Bruce McMillan

Marshall Cavendish New York

For the Red Fox

Late Summer, Northern Iceland

Gletta was only months old when I photographed her in windy Iceland. Her Icelandic name means frolicsome and full of play. She was born at the seaside farm Fagranes, only fifty miles south of the Arctic Circle. Her color, skewbald, is a multicolor of white and deep brown. When full-grown she will be about 13 hands tall, a size considered a pony in most of the world. To an Icelander this small-stature sturdy breed is proudly considered a horse. There are 60-80,000 horses in Iceland, about one for every four Icelanders. This is one of the highest horse-per-person populations in the world.

This book was made possible with the generous help and assistance of:
Einar Gustavsson, the Iceland Tourist Bureau; Debbie Scott and Margrét Hauksdóttir, Icelandair; Þórunn Reynisdóttir, Icelandair/Hertz Car Rental; Vigfús Vigfússon, Hótel Áning, Sauðárkrókur; Jón Eiríksson and his son, Brynjólfur Jónsson, of Fagranes Farm, 551 Sauðárkrókur; and Lori Evans, equine advisor.

The photos were taken in September 1996—often on very breezy days—using a Nikon F4/MF23 with 24, 85, 105 micro, 180 and 300 mm lenses, usually with a polarizing filter when shooting in full sunlight. The 35 mm film, Kodachrome 64, was processed by Kodak in Fair Lawn, New Jersey.

Printed in Italy
First edition printed and bound by Legatoria Editoriale Giovanni Olivotto
Design and typesetting by Bruce McMillan
Type was set in AvantGarde. Text type was set at 24 point.

Marshall Cavendish, 99 White Plains Road, Tarrytown, New York 10591

1 3 5 6 4 2

Library of Congress Cataloging-in-Publication Data

McMillan, Bruce.
Gletta the foal / Bruce McMillan. p. cm.
Summary: An Icelandic foal searches for the source of something she can hear but not see.
ISBN 0-7614-5039-4
1. Iceland horse—Juvenile fiction. (1.Iceland horse—Fiction. 2.Horses—Fiction.) I. Title.
PZ10.3.M1995Gl 1998 (E)—dc21 98-11486 CIP AC

Hi. My name is Gletta.

I was eating grass when…

I thought I heard something.

I looked over here.

I looked over there.

But I didn't see anything making a sound.

I asked my friend if she heard it.

She didn't know what I was talking about.

I heard it again. Maybe Dad knows.

My father said, “It’s okay. We can’t see it.”

I thought, "Something I can't see?"

I asked my uncle but...

he just laughed and said, "I hear it too."

He hears it too? I was scared.

I ran to my mother.

Mom whispered, "Don't be frightened."

I wasn't. I hid behind her.

Mom nuzzled me and said, "Stay with me."

I did. We ate together.

I had an itch I couldn't reach.

Mom helped. Oh, no.

I heard it again. I looked.

I stopped. I wondered.

Mom said, "Come on. Let's go over here."

There it was quiet.

Then it wasn't.

I looked around one last time.

I can hear it? But I can't see it?

I guess it was nothing.

The end.